The Adventures of Moose & Mr Brown

To Pauline (and, of course, Moose, Monty and Mr Brown) – PS

To Amy and Nick – SU

Many thanks to Jeanne Willis for interpreting Paul's words.

First published in the United Kingdom in 2019
by Pavilion Children's Books
43 Great Ormond Street
London, WC1N 3HZ

An imprint of Pavilion Books Company Limited.

Publisher and Editor: Neil Dunnicliffe
Assistant Editor: Hattie Grylls

ISBN: 9781843654285

A CIP catalogue record for this book is available from the British Library.

10 9 8 7 6 5 4 3 2 1

Reproduction by Rival Colour Ltd., UK

Printed by DreamColour Printing Ltd., China

This book can be ordered directly from the publisher online at www.pavilionbooks.com, or try your local bookshop.

The Adventures of Moose & Mr Brown

Paul Smith

illustrations by Sam Usher

PAVILION

I'd like to introduce you to two good friends
of mine.
The first is MR Brown. Like me, MR Brown is a
fashion designer. MR Brown is in charge of
my studio, which is in London's Covent Garden.
He is a gentle boss, he's charismatic, charming
and I look forward to coming to work every
day knowing that he'll greet me with
a smile and a wave!
The second person I'd like to introduce you
to is Moose. I met Moose by chance when
he first arrived in London from Alaska. When
we first met, Moose took an instant
interest in my world of design and creativity.
I was immediately struck by how
curious Moose was and how fascinated
he was by all of the things he
encountered as he went about his day.

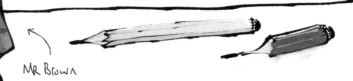

MR Brown

Moose works with Mr Brown in my studio alongside lots of other wonderful characters. My studio is a busy place with lots going on all of the time - the phone never stops ringing and the door never stops swinging! The studio is jam-packed full of things - everything from toys to bikes, books to bunnies, and lots and lots of them! Moose and Mr Brown have the perfect temperaments for the busy studio. They find inspiration in everything that surrounds them, and in the busy studio that means there is plenty to inspire them.

I hope you enjoy their story.

Paul Smith

Moose

This is Moose's passport photo...

...and this is Monty's.

Or is it the other way round? Who knows?

They're identical twins, but Moose is very tidy and organised. And Monty isn't.

You can tell by their baby photos – here they are in their pushchair. Monty is the one upside down…

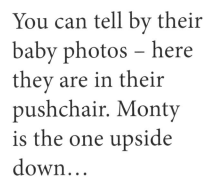

…and this is Monty falling off his potty.

Despite their differences, the twins were very close.

They had never been apart until the day they left Alaska and…

...lost each other at the airport. They were going on holiday to London.

Moose got on the right plane and...

...Monty didn't!

Moose felt so alone without his twin. A tear rolled down his cheek – and *that* was when he first met Mr Brown!

Mr Brown was a famous fashion designer. When he saw Moose looking so sad, he lent him his hanky.

"Sorry to be a cry baby," sniffed Moose, as he explained about losing Monty.

"Not at all," said Mr Brown. "If I lost my brother, I'd need an elephant hanky to dry my eyes."

"An *elephant* hanky?" said Moose. "Is there such a thing?"

Mr Brown whipped out his sketchbook.

"I've designed a whole range," he said. "Elephant hankies for blowing trunks, hippo hankies to wipe muddy nostrils, and that one's for crocodile tears."

"Who is the tiny hanky for?" squinted Moose.

Life Size

"A bumblebee bat," said Mr Brown, waving a magnifying glass.

"She also wants some waterproof clothes to stop the rain going up her nose when she hangs upside down. I'm working on the design in London."

"I'd love to see it," said Moose.

"Then come to my studio," said Mr Brown, "and after that I have to travel for work. If you'd like to keep me company, I'll help you look for Monty."

Moose had never been
to London before.
It was nothing like Alaska.

He'd never seen anything like Mr Brown's studio either.

It was crammed from floor to ceiling with fascinating bits and bobs.

Moose sniffed the air. There was a wonderful whiff of wood, books, cotton and something else – what was it?

"It's called imagination!" said Mr Brown. "Now follow me."

Mr Brown's team were busy working on the
bumblebee bat outfit.
On the desk was a model of a tiny bat wearing
a tiny coat and a tiny hat.

"Perfect!" said Mr Brown. "The coat is rainproof and the hat doesn't fall off. Well done everyone!"

"Mr Brown," said Moose, "if you can make hats for bats, I bet you could make anything for anyone – parkas for penguins, sneakers for cheetahs, scarves for giraffes…"

"What a *brilliant* idea, Moose!" said Mr Brown.

"I'll create a new range of clothes for creatures! Clothes that make their lives better!" he said. "And I want *you* on my team."

"*Me?*" said Moose. "I'd love to! Sunglasses for snakes! Go-faster slippers for sloths! And lots more besides! I'll help you find some new animals to help while we look for Monty."

"Thanks for believing in me, Mr Brown!"

Moose was determined not to let Mr Brown down. When they landed in Japan, he found a flying squirrel who'd lost her tail and couldn't get off the ground.

"Don't worry, I'm sure Mr Brown can design you some trousers with a fluffy tail," said Moose.

And Mr Brown did! The smiling squirrel flew from tree to tree.

"Can you see my twin brother from up there?" called Moose.

But the answer was no.

Monty wasn't in Australia either.

"Sorry, mate," said the kangaroo, "I'm so grateful for the new dungarees, but I've looked everywhere and there's no sign of your brother."

"Never mind, Moose,"
said Mr Brown,
"perhaps we'll have
better luck in...

...New York."

There, Moose found
a skunk who wanted
perfumed pants...

...a bald eagle
in need of a
bobble hat...

…and a bear desperate for snow shoes.

But he couldn't find Monty *anywhere*.

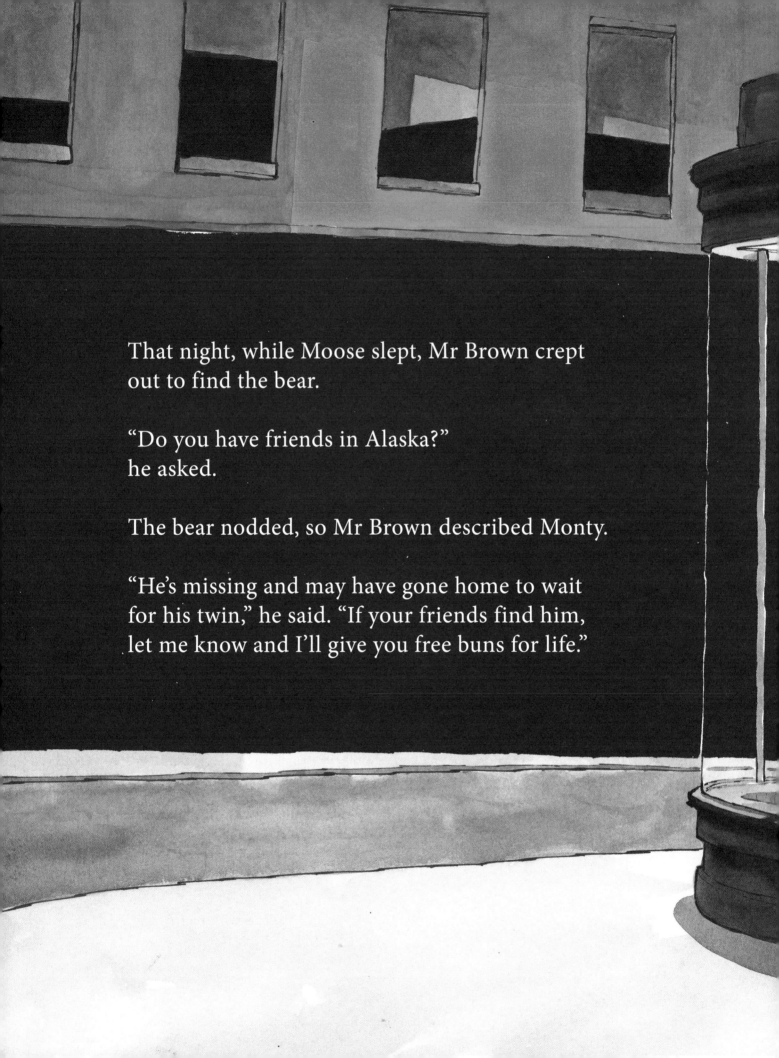

That night, while Moose slept, Mr Brown crept
out to find the bear.

"Do you have friends in Alaska?"
he asked.

The bear nodded, so Mr Brown described Monty.

"He's missing and may have gone home to wait
for his twin," he said. "If your friends find him,
let me know and I'll give you free buns for life."

Next stop, Africa!

The lion was thrilled with his pyjamas, as it was surprisingly cold at night.

The Indian spitting cobra was delighted with his bib...

…and in China, the panda who'd lost her specs *loved* the new ones Mr Brown designed.

"If only Monty were here," sighed Moose, when they arrived in Paris.

"I'm sure he'll turn up," said Mr Brown, smiling.

"To cheer you up, I've reserved a front seat
for you at my fashion show tomorrow."

The queue for Mr Brown's show went around the block. Everyone wanted to know where he got his ideas from.

"I can find inspiration in anything," he said. "This time it came from a marvellous Moose!"

Everyone clapped and cheered when the models hit the catwalk. There was Giraffe, Bear, Panda, Skunk and Snake, all strutting their stuff.

And then...

in the grand finale...

...on marched the world's next top model!

He looked *very much* like Moose, and with a stylish swagger, he twirled ten of Mr Brown's hats on his antlers.

"OH MONTY! MY MONTY!"

Moose cried with joy.

"You found him, Mr Brown! How can I *ever* thank you?"

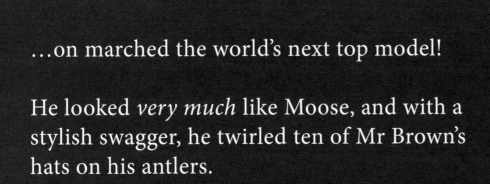

"You already have," grinned Mr Brown.
"You've given me my dream team –
the Moose twins!"